Jess
Illustrations by Maria Akram

The Caterpillar Who Was Afraid to Fly

Bumblebee Books
London

BUMBLEBEE PAPERBACK EDITION

Copyright © Jessica Ruiz 2022
Illustrations by Maria Akram

A CIP catalogue record for this title is
available from the British Library.

ISBN: 978-1-83934-408-4

Bumblebee Books is an imprint of
Olympia Publishers.

First Published in 2022

Bumblebee Books
Tallis House
2 Tallis Street
London
EC4Y 0AB

Printed in Great Britain

www.olympiapublishers.com

Dedication

I dedicate this book to my children, Skye and Sean. May your wings always protect you and you never be afraid to spread your wings and fly.

There was a little caterpillar who lived on the lowest branch of an oak tree with his grandfather. The reason they lived on the lowest branch of the oak tree was because Little Caterpillar had a fear that prevented him from exploring the world around him.

One day Little Caterpillar's grandfather came to him. "Little Caterpillar, today is the day we must part ways, as my journey as a caterpillar needs to come to an end." "But why, Grandfather, where are you going?" asked Little Caterpillar.

"Little Caterpillar, my journey with you as a caterpillar is coming to an end, but I will see you again when you become a beautiful butterfly, and we will fly next to each other in the deep blue sky."

"Fly?" Little Caterpillar asked nervously. "But, Grandfather, you know I can never fly as I have a fear of flying."

"My Little Caterpillar, your fear of flying has hindered your ability to see the world for what it truly is. You cannot live on the ground forever, as the world has many different views to be seen."

Later that night, Grandpa Caterpillar tucked in Little Caterpillar for bed. "Good night, Little Caterpillar, and remember when you awake, I will no longer be here. But I will be waiting for you on top of the tallest oak tree, when you are finally ready to spread your wings and fly."

The next day, Little Caterpillar awoke. Grandpa Caterpillar was gone as he had promised. Little Caterpillar felt so sad and alone. He just knew there was no way he could be brave enough to fly. He left his oak tree in search of what it meant to have courage and be brave.

As little caterpillar walked down the path of the forest, he looked for someone to give him guidance. He saw a little blue bird sitting on top of a hollow tree.

"Little Blue Bird, way up there in that hollow tree, what do you see high above the treetops of the tallest trees?"

"Little Caterpillar, I see the wind whistling as it makes its way through the blissful blue sky and leaves of the trees. I can see the tallest tree touch the clouds way above me."

"But, Little Blue Bird," says the little Caterpillar, "are you not afraid of falling way up there in that hollow tree?"

"Little Caterpillar, do not be silly. What I am most afraid of is not falling, but not being able to use my wings, to sore the highest heights, and see new things."

Little Caterpillar continues his journey to find the courage to fly. When he spots a hummingbird hovering over a garden in the valley tops.

"Little Hummingbird, tell me what do your wings allow you to see hovering over that garden as still as can be?"

"Little Caterpillar, I see flowers in every color of the sea. I see them grow tall and as strong as they can be. I see the rosiest red rose, and a perfect snow-white tulip sunbathing in the sun's rays."

"But, Little Hummingbird, are you not afraid your wings will get tired, hovering over the garden tops?

"Little Caterpillar, do not be silly. My wings help guide me to the places I want to be. Without my wings, I would not be free to travel to the places I want to see.

Little Caterpillar still is not convinced he wants to be a butterfly. The thought of flying still frightens him. It is getting late. The moon is starting to glisten, as he continues to find his courage to fly, when he notices a bumble bee, buzzing around a land of water.

"Little Bumble Bee, I see you buzzing around that water sparkling beneath your wings. What do your wings allow you to see way up there above the shimmering water tops?"

"Little Caterpillar, I see a land of water that is so perfectly calm and still, it clearly mirrors the sky above me, with all the colors of the stars reflecting at me."

"But, Little Bumble Bee, are you worried your wings are not as strong as they seem?" "Oh, little Caterpillar, what I am most worried of is not being able to use my wings, to see all the beautiful things the world has to offer me."

It is getting dark and cold. It is almost time for Little Caterpillar to go into his cocoon where he will gain his wings to fly. But Little Caterpillar still does not think he is brave enough to fly high in the sky.

Little Caterpillar runs into an elderly wise owl sitting on the rooftop of an old barn. "Excuse me old wise owl," whispered Little Caterpillar. "What do you see on the rooftop of that old barn?"

"Little Caterpillar, do you want to know what I see sitting on the rooftop of this barn? I see a scared little caterpillar seeking guidance from me. I understand you are afraid to gain your wings and fly, as high as the sky can see. But your bravery you seek does not come from the little blue bird sitting in the hollow tree, the hummingbird hovering over the garden still as can be, or the bumble bee buzzing around the clear crystal waters."

"Then, Old Wise Owl," pleaded little caterpillar. "please tell me, where does my bravery come from?"

"It comes from within you. Inside you is enough bravery to be all you can be. It is now time, Little Caterpillar, to face your fears and gain your wings."

The Little Caterpillar knew the old wise owl was right. It was now time to face his fear. The Little Caterpillar goes back home to the bottom branch of his oak tree. He hangs upside down and spins himself into a silky cocoon.

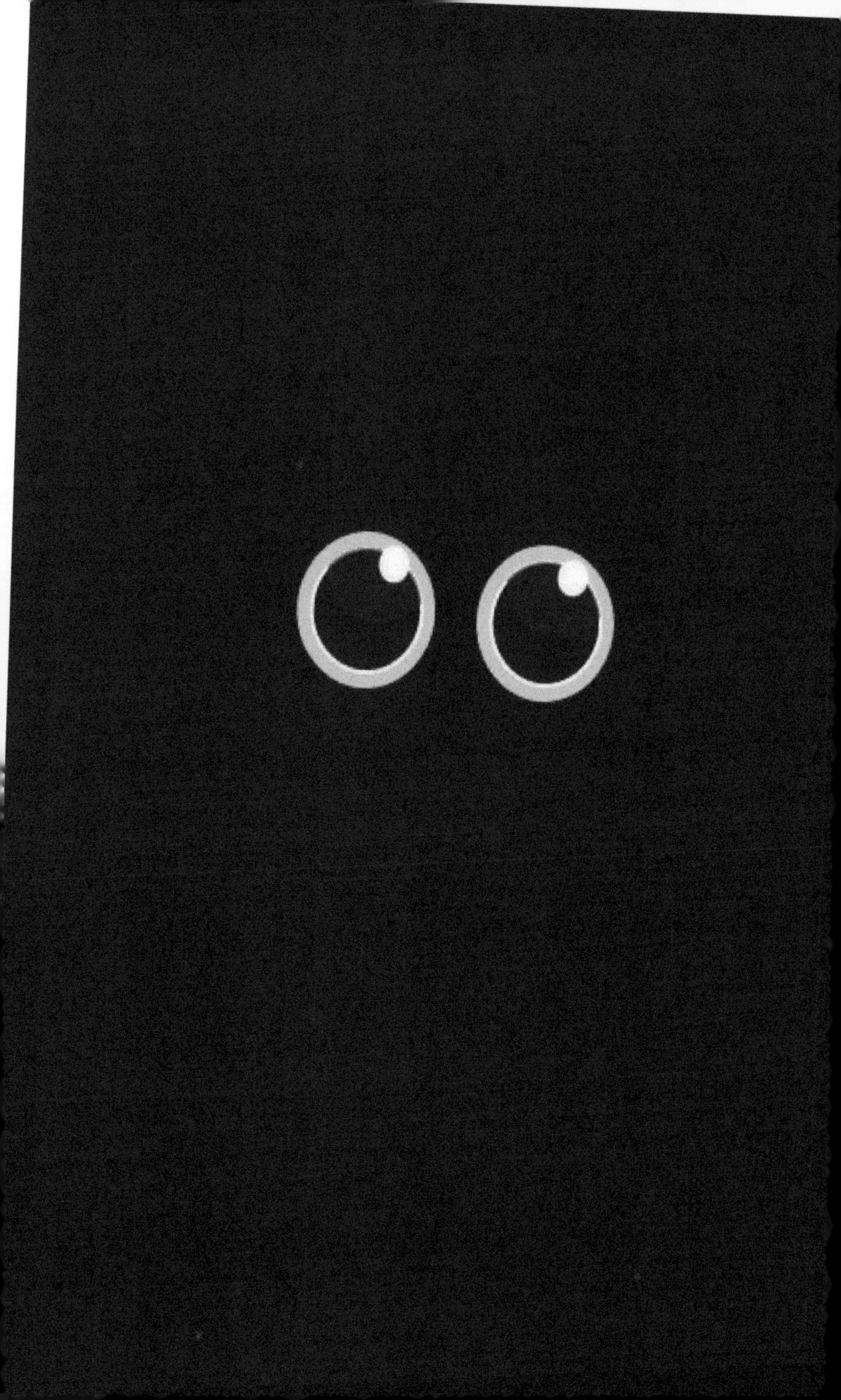

Little Caterpillar sleeps in his cocoon day and night for eight days straight. On the ninth day, Little Caterpillar awakens inside his cocoon. It is dark and tight inside. Little caterpillar tries to move but there is no room. He knows now is the time to see if his wings are as strong as they need to be. On the count of three little caterpillar pushes his way out of the silky cocoon.

One ...

Two...

Three…

With a deep breath he closes his eyes and flaps his wings with all his might. When he opens his eyes, he is at the top of the tallest oak tree and waiting for him is a beautiful butterfly sitting on the tallest branch of the tree. "Grandpa?" asked the little butterfly? "Yes, Little Butterfly, it is me. I see you found the courage to be all you can be." Little butterfly looked at his magnificent new wings. He felt strong and powerful, a feeling he never felt before. He flew next to his grandpa on the tallest branch of the tree.

"Come on, Grandpa," said Little Butterfly.

"Come and fly with me."

"We have the world to see."

About the Author

Jessica Ruiz has been an early childhood educator since 2010. Her love of children's books comes from her many years of reading to young children while she worked for both private and public sector day care facilities. She lives in Germany with her two children, Skye and Sean, and her dog, Cali. Jessica has a masters degree in Early Childhood Education Curriculum and Instruction.

Acknowledgements

I want to thank my parents, Rick and Gaby, for always believing in me no matter what! Thank you to Maria Akram for teaching me the way and for illustrating this book for me.

Printed in the USA
CPSIA information can be obtained
at www.ICGtesting.com
LVHW061213210124
769429LV00057B/1078

9 781839 344084